The New Baby

By Esther Wilkin
Pictures by Eloise Wilkin

Formerly titled *Baby Dear*

A GOLDEN BOOK • NEW YORK

Western Publishing Company, Inc.
Racine, Wisconsin 53404

Baby Dear is my brand-new baby doll.
Daddy brought her to me on a very special day.

It was the day he brought Mommy and our new baby home from the hospital.

Mommy loves her baby.
And I love mine.

We give our babies their bottles.

Then we pat their backs
to bubble them.

Mommy changes her baby.

And I change mine.

Mommy bathes her baby. And I bathe Baby Dear.

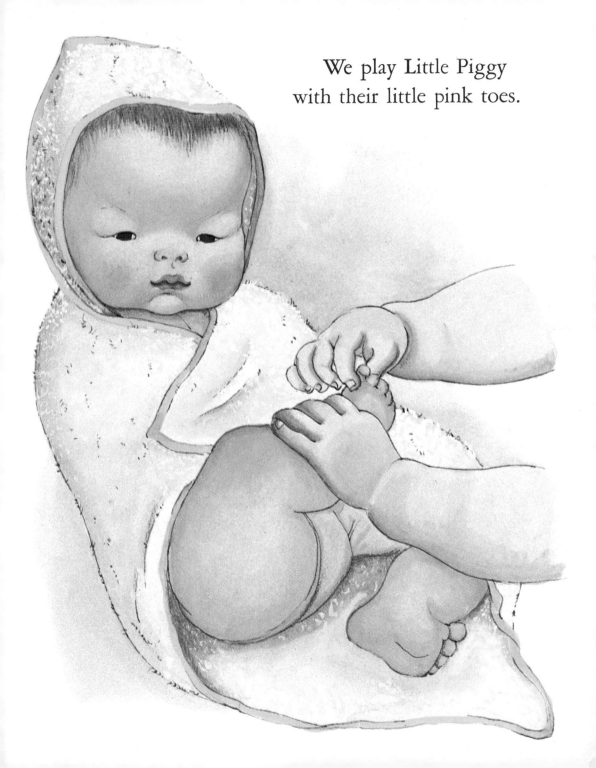

We play Little Piggy
with their little pink toes.

We dress our babies in their bonnets
before we take them out.

Mommy has a carriage for her baby.
And I have one for Baby Dear.

We go walking together with our babies.

Mommy's baby sleeps in the little white bed
that used to be mine.

My baby sleeps in a cradle all her own.

Mommy has a book
for her baby and I have
one for Baby Dear.

We write things in our books about our babies.

Mommy sings to her baby and I sing to mine.

We smile at our babies and talk to them.
Mommy says this is the way our babies know
they are the most wonderful babies in the world.

Sometimes Mommy lets me hold her baby.
Mommy's baby is my baby sister.

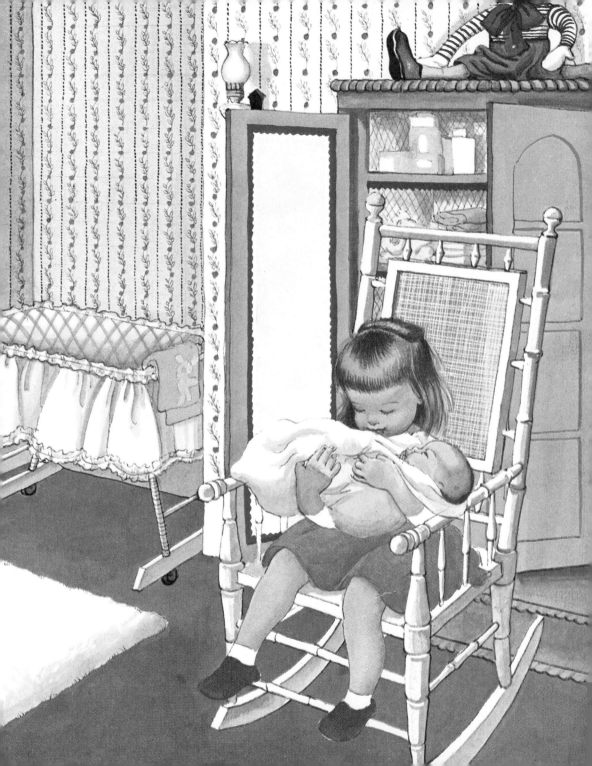

When my baby sister is a big girl
I will let her hold Baby Dear.